Remember.

Remember, it's important.

She said so.

Keep hold of everything.

How did I feel?

SENSELESS

STEVE COLE

With illustrations by
Neil Evans

Barrington Stoke

First published in 2017 in Great Britain by
Barrington Stoke Ltd
18 Walker Street, Edinburgh, EH3 7LP

www.barringtonstoke.co.uk

A CIP catalogue record for this book is available
from the British Library upon request

ISBN: 978-1-78112-733-9

Printed in China by Leo

CONTENTS

CHAPTER 1

Sweet Smell of Success

Wow.

To get off that private jet and have the sunlight dazzle your eyes ... to feel the island heat prickle your skin. The airfield was right next to the sea – you could hear the waves crash and taste the salt on the breeze as it blew in across the wide-open ocean.

Seriously. WOW.

I walked across the airfield with the four other winners towards a cluster of black limousines. The drivers stood by the cars, in dark suits and dark glasses. One of the drivers held up a card with my name on in big, black capitals –

KENZIE 'K-BOY' MITCHELL

I felt a swell of pride. K-Boy had earned this trip. No one had helped him.

It was all down to me.

And how had I won it?

That's the sickest part.

I only won it cos I'm such a totally awesome gamer.

"You're wasting your life playing video games all day and night." That's what they all said. "Almost no kids turn pro at e-sports. Sixteen years old and you're going nowhere."

Nowhere, huh? Well, lick it up, losers!

Who's gone to a sun-soaked paradise island to spend three days playing Sensia State's brand-new console? And who's the one sipping ice-cold OJ in *an actual limo* on his way to a five-star hotel because he kicked serious butt-cheek in the beta-test tournaments?

Me, that's who. K-Boy.

"Don't mind if I do," I murmured, as the driver drove us into the grounds of Sensia State's HQ. It looked like a mini city, with office blocks, shops and streets lined with houses.

"How many people get to live here?" I asked my driver.

"Up to 1,500 people, sir," he said, nice and respectful. "Pretty much all of the Sensia State workers."

"Nice," I said. "I guess this place is a bit far out for people to travel to and from work each day."

"It is," the driver said, then he loosened up a little, just like I'd hoped he would. "Plus, the projects they work on are beyond top secret. The bosses can't risk anyone from the outside world finding out what goes on here ..."

"It's where the magic happens," I said, and I wasn't trying to suck up. The Sensia UltraState is like *proper* magic – like no other console I've played.

Forget virtual reality. The Ultra gives you reality with go-faster stripes. Like, a whole higher level of life.

'And now K-Boy's up high with it,' I thought, as we drove along the perfect grey stripe of road. The leather of the car seats smelled as expensive as it looked, and felt as soft as butter. The sea glittered through the tinted windows, a brilliant, radio-active blue.

Up ahead, a stalagmite of glass and steel rose up into the sky. Total style. Red hologram letters shimmered in the sky above it –

HOTEL ESCAPE

All of sudden the limo braked hard and I was flung forward. Some hipster dude – beard, checked shirt and arty tattoos – had walked out in front of us. For a sick second I was sure we were going to splatter him over the road, but we stopped just in time. The hipster didn't even notice. He was staring about blankly, lost in a world of his own. Then three men grabbed him and bundled him back onto the pavement. The hipster never made a sound.

I thought, as always, 'Take a pic and Snapchat it,' and I grabbed for my phone. But, no chance – there was no public Wi-Fi.

What happens at Sensia HQ stays at Sensia HQ.

"Someone should've gone easy on the free drinks at the hotel," the driver said, and looked back at me, his shades shining sunlight. "Just wait till you see what it's like in there. Your mind's going to blow, kid. Totally blow."

CHAPTER 2

Touch the Dream

I stepped from the limo into crazy heat, then into the shadow of Hotel Escape. Tiredness had crept up on me. Back home it was midnight, but here it was only six p.m.

'So this is what jet lag feels like!' I thought, as I rubbed my eyes. I'd have to get used to long flights when I turned pro. Dreamhack in Sweden, QuakeCon in the US of A, Fragapalooza in Canada ...

K-Boy was going to be mixing with the *big* boys.

The driver pulled my luggage from the boot like it weighed nothing and the hotel's glass doors slid open. I stepped inside.

What I saw refreshed me right away. Wow.

The massive lobby was cool in every way. It was made of nothing but metal and glass and you could have stood a rocket in there. Sparks of light – like fireworks frozen mid-blast, high above us – gave the space a soft glow while steel blinds turned the sun into thick bars of light.

The floor was a grid of white marble and soft grey carpet. As I crossed it I felt like a counter in a board game. Ha, board games! Prehistoric next to what I could see bang centre in the lobby – a Sensia UltraState play-pod, the size of a sports car, pulsing green and good to go.

First instinct – go play.

But the pod had ropes all round it. And there were cameras in the walls, keeping beady electronic eyes on the place. Damn. I wanted to get inside that bubble of plastic. No headset or gloves. Just a wireless patch stuck on your forehead. The big suits at Sensia say it uses 'ultra-haptic technology', holograms, ultrasound and a ton of new inventions that steer your senses. You stand on the track-stand and call out "Start!" – then you open your eyes and you're inside the game.

And you're like, "Whoa. How'd I get here?"

One time, I played this UltraState strategy-shooter game *Pokko*, short for 'apocalypse'. It starts off in this ruined city, and you're there, man. You're just *there*. As you walk, you step on rubble. You smell burning, so real it makes you choke. You hear scuttling animals, creeping footsteps. When you blow apart a zombie, you feel the blood and gore splat on your skin and your ears ring with the *boom* of gunfire. You eat to boost your energy and power, and you can taste the food. I swear I felt it going down into my stomach. That bit made me feel sick. They don't have that bit down quite right yet.

So why was the pod roped off?

That green glow and the hum of power called me so hard. My whole body longed to play the UltraState again. I couldn't wait to get back into that other world where I was a hero, not a zero. There I had proper power – my instincts, my decisions, my reactions ...

My world.

'Get it together, K-Boy,' I told myself. 'You'll be playing big tomorrow.'

Meantime, I had to admit, the Hotel Escape was a pretty good reality.

The guy at the reception desk had a smile as cool and sharp as his suit. "Checking in, sir?"

11

"S'right."

"Here for the Ultimate Contest?"

"Here to smash it," I said with a swagger.

At that, he smiled even sharper. "Lot of people here saying that."

"Yeah, well. I mean it."

A steely voice behind me – *"Even when you don't know the competition?"*

CHAPTER 3

Taste of the High Life

I turned to find this girl like a big "Oh, yeah?" in my face.

Shades on. Hair razored and quiffed. Mean lips. I couldn't help but clock the white patch from her cheek to her neck on her otherwise clear black skin.

Cool.

But I could be cool too. I shrugged. "What competition?"

She smirked. "You're looking at it. Blink."

I blinked, like, super slow.

"My *name's* Blink."

I was sure I could see her roll her eyes behind her shades.

"You?" she said.

"K-Boy."

"Pro?"

"Gonna be."

Blink smirked and pushed her tongue against her teeth. "Sure, we're all *gonna* be, K-Boy. But it's kind of weird, right? There are no big gamers here."

"Get real." I looked about at the little groups in the lobby. "A gig like this, there's got to be?"

"It's a new generation of consoles for a new generation of gamers," the receptionist guy butted in. "Sensia don't want old-school players who made their names on *regular* games. We want tomorrow's stars. That's why you're here."

"That's how Sensia work, right?" Blink looked at me, as if I knew the answers. "They're big on control."

"Control is everything." The receptionist looked at us like we were old friends. "You're smart. You understand that."

I nodded and smiled – yeah, course I got that – and then a waiter honed in on us with a tray of glasses filled with dark, sparkling liquid.

"Your free drinks."

Blink turned up her nose. "I don't do fizzy."

"It's a unique drink rich in rare minerals." The waiter sounded like she'd said this a few times before. "It'll sharpen your game. Give you the edge."

I took a glass. The drink smelled gross, kind of metallic. But the weird thing was, as I sipped, the smell went. I could feel bubbles popping on the end of my nose, but nothing else.

"Drink up," the waiter said, her smile as glossy as her speech. "Everyone else is."

She moved away. I took a gulp. I couldn't taste anything.

Blink did the same and wrinkled her nose. "Ugh, that is rank," she almost spat.

"Can't taste it." I took another, more careful sip. "Thing is, how can this pop give any of us an edge, if everyone's drinking it?"

"Well, I'm *not* everyone." Blink shrugged and tipped her drink into a silver plant pot behind her. "I don't need this to beat the opps. I'm all about the first attack. Get past that and I've got a late-game strategy waiting in the wings." She stuck out her tongue at me. "Maybe someday, someone will do well enough against me to find out what that is."

"Uh-oh," I murmured.

The waiter was back with another drink. "Don't tip the drink away, Theresa." She grinned at Blink. "It will enhance your natural skills – not help that palm tree grow."

Theresa? I smirked and stuck my tongue out at her. "Yeah, drink up nicely, *Theresa*."

"My name is *Blink*." She downed her drink in one go, slammed the glass on the tray, and gave the waiter a '*happy now?*' smile. The waiter nodded and walked away. Only then did Theresa

hold her stomach like she might vomit. "Jeez, what is IN this stuff?" she spluttered. Not so cool now.

I swigged my own drink down but still couldn't taste it. I turned to Blink. "How'd she know your name, *Theresa*?"

Blink didn't rise to it. "Got a big rep, right? Even the staff know who I am."

Maybe that was true. But what I'd seen was that the waiter carried a clipboard as well as her drinks tray. She looked at it again as she went to get two more drinks for her next victims.

I had the feeling she maybe knew everyone's names, rep or no rep.

So, anyway, I hung out with Blink for a bit, and she knew these other guys who seemed sound. I thought the trip was only for the best of the best but it turned out everyone who'd taken part in the Betas was here, even the bottom-of-the-ladder guys. Must've cost Sensia a fortune.

Blink and her new squad left after a bit, when one of those bottom-of-the-ladder types – this girl called Squirrel – came over.

"SQUIRREL, COS I'M NUTS, YEAH?" she kept saying.

But she had red hair and chubby cheeks so that most likely explained the name. I reckoned she should've called herself Hyena cos she kept laughing really loudly at anything and everything.

In the end I dumped her on this dude from Seoul with silver-tipped hair. She got busy telling him how she was planning to hack into the Wi-Fi so she could kick his ass on *Team Fortress 2*.

I left them to it and headed for my room. I was tired, and my head hurt, and the drink sat weird in my stomach. It felt like when you eat on the UltraState, like it's not quite going down.

Still, apart from the dodgy drinks, the hotel was top. The carpet was as soft as the lights. A sweet smell like vanilla hung in the air. I saluted to CCTV cameras on the walls and went to my room on the fourth floor.

And what a room.

Totally sick. All in white. Bed bigger than my whole bedroom back home. Carpet so deep I kind of sunk into it up to my ankles. One wall was all glass and from the balcony I could see across the island to the indigo shadows of the sea.

I thought I'd be so excited I'd be up all night, but you know what? I fell asleep in my jeans, T-shirt and trainers, and with the lights on too. Everything was so soft – the bed, the pillows – that as I lay there, I felt like I was floating. It was like I was lying on air.

I remember the last thing I thought was, 'Tomorrow is gonna be so cool.'

It was later, in the middle of the night, when I was jolted from sleep.

It was then that I heard the screaming from next door.

Don't let the memories fade.

Remember. Keep remembering.

The girl.

*Remember what
happened to that girl.*

CHAPTER 4

Hearing Things

There was a girl screaming next door.

It was weird because when I woke up everything was dark. I knew I'd left the lights on, so how could it be dark? Power cut?

I couldn't see anything. But the girl's screams were loud and clear.

I worked out that she must be on the balcony, shouting on the other side of the glass. That's why I could hear her so well.

"*Help! I can't see!*" she shouted. "*Can anyone hear me? I can't hear myself, I don't know if my voice works ...!*"

Jeez! Her voice worked big-style to my ears. Maybe she was having a bad dream?

I got up – how could it be so pitch black? I felt my way along the wall to find the light switch. *There.* I clicked it on and off but it made no difference. I was shaky and starting to freak now. I stumbled over to the window.

I still couldn't make anything out.

"*I can't see!*" the girl's voice shouted.

Dread swelled inside me, like a wave of ice-cold water. 'You can't have gone blind, this has to be a power cut,' I told myself. But if that was the case, my eyes should be getting used to the dark now.

Truth was, I could see nothing at all.

"Hello?" I called to the girl next door. "I can't see either, are you OK?" Then I remembered – *duh* – she'd said she couldn't hear herself. So how could she hear me?

What should I do?

Call Reception. Someone there will help.

I scrambled about trying to reach the phone, blinking and rubbing at my eyes, willing my sight to return.

Then I heard the door next door open. A man's voice, and a woman's, under the girl's shouts. Help was here. Someone else must've heard her.

But the girl just screamed even louder. "*Who's that? Get off me!*"

I listened, breath held, as the girl struggled and struggled.

"She's a goner," an American voice said, deep and sullen.

"Put her to sleep," the woman's voice said in reply.

To sleep? I'm telling you, I was ready to wet myself by now. *No way, they can't be serious.*

"What are you doing?" The girl's voice was tight with terror. "No ... no ..."

Her voice was fading, getting fainter. Sleepy. What had they done to her?

"I hoped we'd found a miracle," the man said. "It hasn't worked."

"It was always a risk," the woman retorted. I knew that voice – she was the waiter who'd forced the drinks on us in the lobby. "But the state needs pushing along if –"

"She was pushed over the edge!"

"It's bad luck," our waiter said calmly. "We'll put her in the pile for disposal."

Pile? Disposal?

I stood, frozen. Nothing made sense. I didn't feel safe at all. Plus I couldn't see, and what I could hear was insane …

What the hell was going on around here?

A moment later, a burst of static exploded in my head. I cried out. I could see again – but everything was too bright, like there were spotlights shining out of my eyes. My focus was shot. I fell over, and sank into soft carpet.

"Listen!" the waiter said from the balcony. "That was the boy next door. Kenzie Mitchell."

I tried to stay silent. Tried to calm my breathing. I tasted vomit in my mouth as my sight flashed and flickered. It was like someone was pulling on a cable that plugged my eyes into my head. I bit my lip, willed myself not to groan out loud.

"It's all gone quiet now. Maybe he'll sleep through this," the deep voice said. "The morning staff can sort him out, along with the others. We'd better get this girl away for sign-off."

I lay there, still, like I was paralysed, as I tried to make sense of everything. My sight was getting back to normal, but how had it just switched off like that? I remembered how I couldn't taste the drink last night, although Blink said it was rank.

What was happening to my senses?

Was I going crazy?

I lay there on the carpet for ages, checking and re-checking that everything made sense. The lights were off, and the stars outside were bright, but blurred by the long sheer curtains at the window. I could feel the room's white luxury and soft carpet all around in the soft shadows. I couldn't hear anything now.

Somehow the silence was louder than the screams.

Then I heard a sound – someone was outside my door. The handle slowly turned.

No way! I had locked the door before I went to bed, right? No one could just walk in from outside, right?

Except for the people who'd just walked in on the girl next door and dragged her away.

I lay still, frozen, as the door pushed open. A dark figure crept in.

CHAPTER 5

Doubt Your Eyes

I narrowed my eyes and tried to act asleep. But my eyelids flickered like crazy. From between my lashes I saw the dark figure step into my room and creep up on me.

'What do I do?' I thought. 'Why did I shout out like that?'

The figure bent over me. A hand shook me. I didn't react.

Then I heard the figure speak. "Not you too," she said.

My eyes snapped open. "Blink?"

Blink gasped then fell back and banged her head on the wall. "Goddammit, K-Boy!"

"What're you doing here?" I hissed.

"I'm here to check on you. This place has gone crazy." Blink rubbed the back of her head. "You OK?"

"I couldn't see for a bit," I said.

"Me neither." Blink looked upset. "Some people have it worse. Doctors ... well, I thought they were doctors ... they just injected them, took them away for –"

"For ... disposal?"

Blink stared at me. "You heard it too?"

"It must be a ... I dunno, slang word for taking someone to hospital."

'Yeah, Kenzie,' I thought, 'that's the total truth – not.'

"See ..." I told her. "A man and a woman came for the girl next door ..."

I told Blink the lot. Even about the hipster who'd stepped out into the road in front of my limo. I knew now – he'd stepped out cos he couldn't hear the engine, couldn't see the car. Didn't know where he was.

He just knew he had to get away.

"*Someone should've gone easy on the free drinks at the hotel,*" the driver had said, with a laugh.

As Blink listened she looked down at the floor, and her fingers stroked the white patch on her cheek.

"They heard me ... make a noise," I finished. No way could I tell Blink how I'd shouted out like a little kid. "But they didn't come in. They said the morning staff would sort me, along with all the others."

"Well, no one's sorting me." Blink stood up. She was fully dressed, like I was. "I reckon all this has got something to do with that drink they gave us."

"A drink that makes you blind?" I scoffed, then hesitated. "I kind of lost my sense of taste ..." I said. "But why would anyone bring us all the way out here to mess us up with a drink?"

Blink shrugged. "Why bring us out here at all?"

"Duh." I shrugged back at her. "We won this trip."

"Grow up, K-Boy. For the Betas, everyone took the train or bused it to the game-centres to compete. They never told us then that we'd won."

Blink went on, "And it's not just winners here, is it? Sensia has flown out pretty much everyone who took part. There's loads of us here. Why?"

"Oh, shut up! It's a games company," I said, "not, like, gangsters who want to kidnap a bunch of random kids."

"But we're not random, are we?" she insisted. "We all played those Sensia trials. We're all stuck here – no matter if we won or we lost. On our own. Out of the way ..."

Now she was creeping me out.

"*I hoped we'd found a miracle*," that man had said. "*The state needs pushing along ...*"

The girl next door had sounded like she was in a total panic.

Wait. Wait a minute.

Sounded.

"I know what this is," I said.

I hadn't seen anything. I'd only overheard them talk. Crazy guess work and imagination filled in the gaps.

Blink looked at me, her arms folded. "Well?"

"It's a L.A.R.P.! They've set up a L.A.R.P. for us."

Blink stared at me. "L.A.R.P. as in – Live-Action-Role-Play. As in we run around the place pretending we're in a real adventure?"

"Duh! Of course. Man, it's so obvious!"

"For real?" She put out her hand to pull me to my feet. "I woke up blind, K-Boy. I tried to call Reception for help. Next thing I know this man's here, talking nice, telling me it's gonna be all right. Then my sight, like, turns on again and I see he's no doctor. He's dressed like a soldier and he's got this massive needle in his hand, gonna put me to sleep." Blink shuddered. "Vik came in and smashed this guy on the head, got me away."

"Slow down," I said. "Who's Vik?"

"Vik for Viking," she told me. "Guy I met last night. He lost his sense of touch and his hearing. He was scared to death. Said he fell out into the corridor and saw soldiers dragging people out of rooms in body bags."

"Yeah, and what else?"

"One of the soldiers chased him. Vik knocked him out, took his swipe card."

I snorted. "This kid beat up a soldier?"

"Vik's not a kid." Blink looked at me like I was nothing. "He couldn't feel any pain, could he? Didn't know how hard he smashed the guy. Anyway, he tipped the guy down some steps. Then he went to look for others to help."

"Sure he did – cos he's one of the game crew, that's why he wants to round up players into teams to make the role-play start."

"But ..." Blink stopped for a second. "He said we should find anyone else who's OK and get them up on the roof –"

"Yeah, to get us all in one place, so Vik can tell us our mission, start us on the game." I was feeling confident now. I'd got it sussed. "Don't you see? That's why all the losers are here too – to set the game up for us winners, who get to play!"

"Maybe ... you could be right." Blink looked glad, but angry too. "I've been scared to death. Going blind like that ... then the soldiers ... it was so *real*."

"This is Sensia. They're all about the reality, right? The control." I nodded. I was sure now that it was all a game. "Bet it *was* the drink that punched out our senses."

"Let's just get to the roof," Blink said. "When we find Vik, I've got a few things to say to him."

I led the way out into the corridor. We crept along to the door to the stairs. I clocked the security camera near by. It was smashed.

"Guilty," Blink whispered. "That was me. God, I hope I don't have to pay for it."

Then we heard a loud groan from the other side of the door.

Here we go! Game on ...

I smiled as I gripped the handle and opened the door a crack. Blink was right behind me.

An Asian-looking dude lay sprawled on the stairs. My age, maybe. He was shaking and crying. Blood leaked from a crack in his head. It

40

looked real, not at all like make-up. Maybe he'd fallen. The waiter from last night, the woman I'd heard in the room next door, was next to him.

But she wasn't dressed like a waiter now. She was in a black jumpsuit with blue flashes.

Proper Soldier Girl.

"I can't hear nothing," Cracked Head Dude sobbed.

"It's too late for you," said Soldier Girl.

She pulled out a syringe. I watched, feeling ill, as she pushed the needle into Cracked Head Dude's neck and pressed the plunger. His body twisted. Eyes and veins bulged, like they were ready to pop.

Then he fell still. His breath stopped.

My confidence crumbled away to dust. This was no role-play. Soldier Girl didn't know we could see her.

The waiter who'd smiled as she'd served my drink last night had just killed this guy.

I felt dizzy, sick. I lost my balance, leaned on the door. It opened with a soft squeak.

Soldier Girl turned and looked up, straight at us.

CHAPTER 6

On the Scent

"You. Your name's Kenzie, isn't it?" Soldier Girl got up, dropped the needle on Cracked Head Dude's body. "Can you see me?"

I didn't answer. I was too scared. Frozen stiff.

She tried again. "Which senses have you lost?"

"This is all a game, right?" I croaked out the words. "A game."

Soldier Girl looked lost for a moment, but then she smiled. "Yes, that's right. It's a game. Come here and I'll tell you the rules."

Yeah, right.

I stepped back from the door and it closed. I heard her footsteps as she came after us.

"Run," I told Blink.

"You run," she hissed back.

A moment later and the door burst open. I *did* run, then, as Soldier Girl charged out at us.

Blink ambushed her. She came at her from the side and slammed her against the wall, then landed a fist in her face. Soldier Girl's head banged off the wall and she sank to the floor.

"What's going on?" Blink was all up in her face. "What have you done to us?"

Soldier Girl couldn't answer. She was out cold, blood tanking from her nose.

"Hey." I crossed over to Blink. "You, like, destroyed her."

"Told you last night." Blink stared down at Soldier Girl on the floor. "I'm all about the first attack."

"Yeah, impressive. But she can't tell us anything now."

"She can still make a point." Blink pulled a full needle from Soldier Girl's hand and passed it to me. "And you can defend yourself with this. I'm gonna check on that guy on the steps."

She slipped out the door. I looked around. My nerves jangled. It was dead quiet, just Solider Girl's uneven breath. I shuddered at the size of the needle in my hand and sniffed at the pale yellow liquid inside. I couldn't smell a thing.

That was when I realised with a chill that the corridor's vanilla smell had gone too.

Another sense down.

I jumped as Blink came back, her eyes full of tears. "He's dead, Kenzie. Proper dead. Role-play game, my big fat –"

The rest I couldn't hear.

Hearing had snapped off now as well as smell.

What?

I dropped the needle, grabbed my head with both hands. I could feel my jaw move and my tongue in my mouth, but there was no sound. It was like the world had turned to silent. I felt a sick lurch of panic.

Blink was suddenly beside me, her face full of worry. She pointed up, mouthed a word at me.

"*Roof.*"

Just like Vik had said.

In a daze, I followed Blink up the stairs. I couldn't hear our footsteps. The silence was total. The only noise was inside my head – my thoughts and the shouts of the girl next door and Cracked Head Dude's groan replayed at random.

We reached the top of the stairs. Blink pulled a gold card from her pocket and swiped it in the card reader on the door. A red light winked to green and Blink pushed the door open.

We were on the roof – it was a white concrete jetty next to the deep blue sea of the night. The red letters HOTEL ESCAPE floated above us.

Then I cried out as a hard electric *crunch* seemed to split my head. I screwed up my eyes as sound came in hard, brutal spurts. Now it was like there was a loose wire from a speaker in my head and something was trying to rip it out.

I felt my knees give way, and then the concrete bite into them as they hit the roof. The pain made me gasp, and I heard it this time.

Blink was up in my face. "You back?"

"Hearing's back." I nodded. "Just can't smell anything. The way I'm bricking it, that may be a good thing."

Then I looked behind Blink and saw a guy with a beard in a black Star Wars T-shirt, long blond hair, maybe 18 or 19. He looked like a skinny Thor who'd gone two rounds with the Hulk – bumps and cuts down his face and arm. Maybe his story of his fight was true.

He helped me up. "I'm Vik."

Like I didn't know. "K-Boy," I told him.

"Blink," Vik asked her, "is he the only one you found?"

"We ran into trouble," she said. "Waiter from last night killed a guy."

I shivered. "You sure he was dead?"

Blink glared at me. "K-Boy reckons this could all be a L.A.R.P., a role-play game."

"Let him," Vik said, "if that stops him freaking out."

"I'm not deaf just now," I said. "OK, say this *is* real. Is hiding on the roof such a good plan? We can't escape, can we?"

Vik's face turned hard. "This place is swipe-card protected. They won't think we can get up here, so they won't look."

"What about when that guy you clobbered wakes up and finds his swipe card gone?"

"I can hit hard." Vik said it like a warning. "And when your senses can all break down any moment, this is the safest place. Want to go it alone? Feel free."

"Free!" I wanted to laugh. I couldn't believe that my amazing, one-off trip had turned into ... well, what? It was more than a nightmare.

It was a killing ground.

Blink broke the silence. "Squirrel getting anywhere?"

"Squirrel?" I asked.

I looked around and saw someone in the neon red shadow under the word ESCAPE. The nutty girl from the bar was here. She was hunched over her laptop. She stared at the screen and tapped at the keys now and then.

"Is ... is she OK?"

51

"Her senses seem fine," Vik said. "Lucky cow. And lucky for us. She's good. She's hacked into the Sensia server."

So Squirrel wasn't just showing off when we first met. Hacking's not like it looks on films, where people type super fast and code scrolls up the screen at 1,000 miles an hour. I've tried it. In real life you mostly press 'Start' on some software then go for a cup of coffee. I can't be doing with it. I've got no patience.

Squirrel looked up from her work. She looked tired and scared, same as we all did. "Hey, K-Boy," she said, with a nervous giggle.

"Anything?" Vik asked.

"Sensia have a kick-ass firewall to block the outside world. Don't hate me. All I can do is scan the internal servers."

"That's great." Vik sighed. "Perhaps you'll find a memo online, yes? That says why they want us dead."

"How did you get in?" I asked Squirrel.

"I clocked the front desk's log-in when I first got here," Squirrel said. "Filmed him on my phone so I could work out the password and get into Sensia's O.S. Plan was, I'd delete the room service bill of anyone who'd party with me. People don't hang out with me unless there's something in it for them. But guess what I found." Squirrel paused. "That guy on the front desk, he's like, senior admin for Sensia's systems."

"The guy who checked us in is top rank for Sensia?" I frowned. "Why would he be pretending to work in the hotel?"

"He wants to do his own dirty work?" Blink suggested. "He wants to keep stuff to himself."

"Squirrel got into this guy's email," Vik told me. "He sent a message late last night to something called Blue Ops."

"I've got it here, hang on." Squirrel read from the screen. *"Project begun. Subjects ready to assess, collect and dispose of."*

"Soldier Girl's jumpsuit looked like it was Blue Ops ..." I shivered, cold all of a sudden. "Then, this ... isn't a wind-up?"

No one answered.

"Why us?" I went on. "Why here?"

"I'm trying to find out," Squirrel said. "Trust me. This Squirrel is on the scent."

"Obvs, it's to do with the UltraState," Vik said. "We know the console distorts our senses, yes? Maybe there's a bug they didn't know about in the Betas – some bad code that's messed up our minds."

"*Your* minds," Squirrel said. "I'm OK so far."

"Maybe that's why they didn't want to test with the big gamers," Vik said. "Too much bad publicity if something went wrong."

Blink shuddered. "It *has* gone wrong. Big time."

"But it's only messed up a bunch of second-rate players who won't make a fuss," I said. "So that's OK." I shivered again in the heat of the tropical night. I knew that soon someone would find we were gone, find the missing swipe card.

Then they would come after us. To finish what we had helped them start.

"Your mind's going to blow, kid."
The driver said that. "Totally blow."

He must've been laughing so
hard behind my back.

Remember.

However dark it gets,
remember.

CHAPTER 7

Feel the Heat

Can you imagine how scared I felt? How *stupid*. I mean, I was the kid who gets in the van with the stranger cos he's promised a sweet. They didn't need to kidnap me. I'd got on a plane and smiled as they dropped me in the lion's den …

I looked out across the night and saw the planes still on the airfield. "They didn't head back to the mainland?"

"I heard there's a hurricane blowing up," Vik said. "The planes can't fly tonight."

"Right," Squirrel said, "and Admin Guy doesn't want the pilots or crew to see something they shouldn't."

"So I guess the pilots aren't staying at Hotel Escape," said Blink. "Where are they?"

Squirrel read an email. "They're sleeping overnight where the staff stay. There's plenty of space, just now. Most of Sensia's workers were given a free holiday this weekend and packed off home."

"So they're out of the way too." I bit my lip. "Sensia must think that the fewer who know what's going on, the better." Every detail made the trick seem more real. And our situation even worse.

But, no. I couldn't afford to think that way. Whatever game I play, I find my strength in my opponents' weakness. I work out someone's weak spot, then play on it until I win.

We just had to work out the weakness here.

"If we can find the pilots," I said, "and tell them what's going on ... Maybe they'll help us get out of here."

Vik shook his head. "They'd never believe us."

"Far as they know, we're all here for the UltraState tournament," Blink added. "They'll think we're stupid kids out to wind them up."

"Hey! The tournament network is set up and good to go in the Video Arena," Squirrel put in. "This email says so."

"That's *so* cool." Blink's voice was full of scorn. "Maybe we can play before they stick their needles of death into us."

"Sorry." Squirrel looked sad. "I was just saying ..."

"I don't understand," I said. "Why did Sensia set everything up, only to move in tonight before the tournament starts?" I frowned. "Hold on. Think about this. The UltraStates are connected over the network, so we can play each other, yeah?"

"You, um, want to *play*, K-Boy?" Squirrel said.

"Point is," I said, "if you can hack into that network direct – from a computer plugged right into it in the Video Arena – then it might be easier to crack their security and find a back way onto the web."

"Then we can shout out for help!" Vik broke in.

"We can film what's going on and post it all over the internet," Blink added.

"We need real proof now to nail Sensia." Vik looked down at Squirrel. "You sure you can't find anything?"

"I'm sorry. I'm trying!" Squirrel peered at the screen. "I told you, even with Admin Guy's password, I can't get to the hot stuff."

"Can you get us off this roof?" I begged.

"All the doors in the hotel can be unlocked at once," Squirrel muttered. "I just need to find a way to make that happen without Sensia knowing."

"And can you do that?" Blink asked her.

"I'm sure I can." Squirrel was typing again, muttering to herself. She stopped, put her hand into her pocket. "Hey, I got nuts from the minibar in my room. Squirrel with her nuts, OK? Anyone want nuts?"

We all just stared at her. She looked back, held out two bags of Honey-Roasted. In the end, I took a handful. I didn't feel hungry, I just felt sorry for her.

The honey roast was salty sweet. Those nuts were pretty good.

Then the flavour vanished. I couldn't taste anything. It was like crunching on chalk.

I spat out the nuts and hugged my knees. The sky was starting to grow light.

I wondered if I'd see the sunrise. Or would my eyes shut down.

Or – would I be dead?

CHAPTER 8

Keep Invisible

Dawn was drowning the stars, turning the blue sky into grey. I was sweating hard. Squirrel's laptop battery was almost gone, its life ebbing away. I knew how it felt.

We'd seen movement in the shadows beyond the hotel. Trucks rumbling to and fro, their loads unknown. Voices rose from the streets around, sharp and shrill, like the call and response of soldiers.

Meanwhile, all of us on the roof of the Hotel Escape stewed in silence. I couldn't keep still. I pressed my tongue to my teeth, waiting for my sense of taste to return. My sense of smell was back but that just meant I knew we all stank of sweat.

Vik sat cross-legged on the concrete, his eyes shut. Blink peered out over the low wall, trying to see what was going on in the gloom below. Squirrel stared on and on. I just wanted to hide from everything and everyone.

Worst. Party. Ever.

"FINALLY! Go, nuts!" Squirrel shouted. Her face was pressed up to her laptop like she was going in for a kiss. "I've unlocked the doors on the staff stairwell. That's our way down."

In a heartbeat Blink was beside her. "You mean, stairs that the hotel guests don't use?"

"Yeah," said Squirrel. "So workers at the hotel can come and go without bothering the people staying here." Squirrel wiped her sweaty hair off her face. "Vik, you got this?"

I looked over at him. His eyes were open, but blank, and he was staring around like the hipster I'd seen in the road.

"I'm blind again," he said. "I'm sorry. Will you ... please lead me –?"

"No problem," Blink told him.

I helped Vik up. I knew how he felt. "You'll get your eyes back," I told him. "But I don't know when –"

"When we see Soldier Girl and her needles?" Squirrel suggested.

"Shut up," Vik snapped. "People are sick and dying, and you think it's a joke?"

"I'm sorry. I didn't mean it. I always say the wrong thing ..." Squirrel was so upset she was all folded in on herself. "Don't hate me, Vik. Don't be mad at me."

"Chill, Squirrel," I said, as I steered Vik and Blink over to a small shed in the far corner of the roof. "We'll stick together. It's thanks to you that we've got a way out of here."

"I've looked at the Sensia HQ plans too," Squirrel went on, always keen to impress us. "Sewers run under all the buildings. We can get to them from the basement and come out in the Plaza, where the Video Arena is."

"Should help us stay invisible a bit longer." Blink waited beside the dark green door to the top of the staff stairs. A sign said –

No Entry!

Staff only!

Stop! Alarm Will Sound!

With a deep breath, Blink yanked the door open.

No alarms went off.

"There." Squirrel nodded. "You may now worship the Squirrel."

"If you get us to the tournament," I said, "I'll worship you for a week."

"*Step this way!*" Squirrel raised her hands in glee.

The stairs were bare concrete, a world away from the luxury on the other side of the wall. As we ran down, our footsteps sounded like thunder. For the 1,000th time, I replayed the scene when Soldier Girl stuck that needle in Cracked Head Dude's neck. An idea bit at the back of my brain again and again. Our senses were all so messed up. How could Blink know for sure that the guy was dead?

Was Blink trying to trick me?

The way our five senses – sight, taste, hearing, touch and smell – were sparking out, it was as if some*thing*, some*body*, was getting inside us and taking bits of us away, then giving them back later ...

Could I trust Vik and Blink and Squirrel at all? I'd seen Soldier Girl inject Cracked Head Dude and it looked like she'd killed him, but then Blink had knocked Soldier Girl out cold. How could I ever know who Soldier Girl really was?

"Not so fast," Vik whispered as Blink steered him down the stairs. There was no one around. I wished that Cracked Head Dude and Next Door Girl would leap out in front of me to yell, "SURPRISE!"

But the shadows were still and dark as Blink led us to a trapdoor set into the concrete floor. This must lead to the sewer tunnels. I lifted the cover and saw a ladder going down into the blackness. It stank of bleach and I was glad of that. 'Sense of smell,' I thought, 'please stick around.'

"You won't be the only one who can't see," I told Vik. "We'll all be in the dark down there."

"My phone's got a torch," Blink said.

She flicked it on and went first down the ladder. She splashed into shallow water and I helped Vik go after her. Squirrel next, and then I went last into the curve of the tunnel. I shivered in my T-shirt, my trainers were soaked in seconds. The smell was horrific and the gloom made me scared that my sight was going. Sound crackled in my ears, like I was ready to spark out again.

"Hold on," I breathed, "please just hold on."

"I just thought," Vik said and his voice sounded hollow. "K-Boy told us this whole crazy thing was a live-action role-play. It's not. But it could still be a game."

"What're you on about?" I said.

"Think about it. Thrown into strange places like this ... coming face-to-face with death, planning our escape." Vik laughed out loud, a spooky flutter of echoes. "We came here to play UltraState. What if the tournament's already started? What if that drink knocked us out and they put us in a play-pod while we slept? What if we're already playing, here and now?"

Oh, Vik.
Oh, man.

We were playing something, all right.

> *(Hold onto that,*
> *hold onto that,*
> *hold onto that,*
> *hold onto that.)*

Remember.

Remember Squirrel.

> *Remember what they*
> *did to poor Squirrel.*

CHAPTER 9

Bright Ideas

"So, you think nothing's real, Vik?" Blink said. "Yeah, right. This is all just a game."

"Come on, UltraState is more real than real." Vik sounded excited – he felt he was close to the truth. "Think about it. These black-outs we're having could be bugs in the player interface."

"But then why am I OK?" Squirrel whispered.

"And the soldiers *know* our senses are buggy," I said. "The bugs are part of the gameplay."

"Yeah, OK. Maybe they are!" Vik agreed. "I bet the game is that we have to find a cure, then find a way off this island. Sensia's testing how we work as a team. The three best players keep losing their senses and must make up for each other – while our weakest member is OK."

"Thanks," Squirrel muttered.

"Kind of easy, the way you found those plans," Blink said. "Like you were meant to. Like it *was* a game."

"You don't know how hard that hack was. I did it all myself. Honest!" Squirrel flinched as Blink turned the torch on her. "Look, I know I'm thick an' all, but how *can* we be in the game? The only play-pod I saw was in the lobby. I know it was switched on, but ..."

"This is Sensia HQ. They're developing new tech all the time," Vik said. "For all we know, the whole of Hotel Escape could be one giant play-pod!"

"You don't just stay in a hotel, you stay in a game," I breathed. "And they flew us out here to test it?" I was starting to think it might just be true. Perhaps this *was* all a game and the game developers were watching us right now. They'd be high-fiving, happy at how clever they were to have tricked us for so long.

"Real or not, we've got to press on, huh?" Squirrel said. "And this Squirrel thinks the manhole above us is the way out onto the plaza."

Blink didn't look sure. "You're the one with all her senses, Squirrel. You go first."

"Thanks," Squirrel said as she climbed the steel ladder on the wall and pushed the manhole cover above her head. "Ugh, squirrels are rubbish at heavy lifting."

"Let me." I climbed the ladder and pressed up next to her, as Blink shone the torch up at the cover. I could smell Squirrel's stale breath, see my reflection in her glasses, see every hair on her bushy eyebrows. She darted forward and kissed me on the cheek.

"For luck," she said, then looked down. She was shaking.

Every little detail ...

It all made my heart sink. No game-world could be this real.

Could it ...?

The metal cover rasped as I lifted it up. I was first to peep out and I blinked in the pale light.

Squirrel was spot on. The plaza was an open expanse of elegant marble, blue glass and steel. It looked as if the pyramids of Ancient Egypt had smashed into the columns of Ancient Rome.

Massive capital letters shone on the biggest pyramid. They declared –

THE VIDEO ARENA

Right now, the plaza was empty.

I helped Squirrel out, and then Vik. He gazed around, still blind.

"I … I think I'm closing down again," he said. "No sight, no taste, no smell … and now my touch too."

"Hey. This is a game, right?" Blink said, as she scrambled out. "Not for ever."

"If I die –" Vik began.

"Shut up," Squirrel said. "You don't win a thing by dying."

I pushed the metal cover back in place. I flinched at how loud the noise seemed in the silence.

"We need to hide," Blink said.

In the base of the Video Arena, two huge glass doors stood open. We crossed over to them. Inside the Arena, I could see a line of UltraState play-pods, screens that filled every wall, each one glowing with the Sensia logo, that black and red snake eating its tail. I felt excitement beat in my chest. If only Squirrel could work her magic again ...

"Wait." Blink froze. "There are loads of people in there."

She was right. Some were slumped in the play-pods. Others were propped up in chairs, their heads pointed to the screens on the walls.

But no one moved. No one stirred. No one spoke.

No one breathed.

"What *is* this?" Blink whispered.

Cold sweat dripped down my back. "I think they're dead."

"What?" Squirrel pushed past us. "*No ...*" she gasped in horror.

Vik grabbed at my arm. "What can you see?"

The screech of tyres cut in before I could tell him. I turned and saw a black open-top jeep, with a bright blue star on its bonnet. It roared into the plaza and braked hard, maybe 100 metres away.

The soldier at the wheel was waving his arm at us, shouting. *"Get away from there, you ...!"*

We'd already started to run. I made for the manhole cover, Squirrel next to me. Blink shouted after us. I stopped, turned, saw her bent over Vik, down on the ground. He was blind, and if his touch was lost too, then he had no contact with the world around him.

Leave him! I wanted to scream.

Instead I yelled at Squirrel, "Get the cover open!" and I ran back to help Blink with Vik. I got him in a kind of piggyback and we ran, me with Vik on top of me.

Blink was just ahead of us. "Where's *he* going?" she panted, staring at the soldier in the jeep.

The jeep was reversing –

Just as the Video Arena exploded.

The noise and power of it was like a volcano erupting. The blast hurled me forward with Vik still on my back. As I hit the ground I saw a storm of fire and glass and steel and smoke blow out from the side of the pyramid.

Squirrel had no time even to scream before the blaze engulfed her.

CHAPTER 10

Lost Your Touch

I don't know how I survived the blast. The air boiled. Shock waves sent me skidding into the blazing blizzard. Out of control, I shrieked with my lungs full of ash. The roar of the blast rang in my ears, then came to a sudden stop as hot blackness took everything away.

But I couldn't have been out for long.

My eyes opened and I saw Vik beside me. His face was like a map with roads drawn in blood. His Viking hair was burned away to black stubble. I pushed myself up on raw elbows and saw that the blast had hit Vik hardest – his clothes were in shreds. He'd been a shield for my back. But his own back looked like a pit of tar.

I was numb to the horror. I saw a twisted heap on the plaza that had to be Squirrel. Poor Squirrel. But Blink …?

"Get up!" She was there with me, struggling to lift Vik. "Quick. The jeep."

Still in shock, I saw the soldier smeared on the ground beside his jeep. The jeep was thick with jagged scars and the seats smouldered. Blink was limping towards it and I went with her. My trainers crunched on glass and rubble, my shoulder hurt as I jammed it under Vik's armpit to get him to the jeep.

"I'm fine," Vik said over and over, his lips bloody. "Got lucky. Blast didn't touch me."

Whoa. He couldn't feel or see or smell a thing.

"Lucky, yeah," I said, my voice shaky. "Blink, can you drive?"

"Sort of." She choked in the smoky air. "C'mon. Gotta get out of here."

"What even happened?" I said. "The Video Arena blew up –"

"It was full of dead bodies, remember?" Blink sounded fierce as anything. "People from the hotel. Sensia had them killed – they're getting rid of the evidence."

"Evidence of what?"

"Of what they've done to us all!"

At last we were at the jeep. The engine was on, and we heaved Vik into the back.

"I don't get it. That soldier died trying to *warn* us." I spat blood on the burned ground. "Why would he want to try to save us?"

"*I don't know!*" Blink screamed. "The UltraState's done something to us. I don't know what, but this is no game."

"It is!" Vik smiled with bloody lips from the back seat. "I'm telling you, we're still inside the game. The UltraState's so hi-tech, you can't tell what's real ... and what's in your head."

I wanted to believe him. But every instinct I had told me he was wrong. "What are we going to do?" I whispered.

"We've got to get to the airfield, find the pilots, hope they'll help us." Blink jumped into the driver's seat. "We'll lose Vik soon ..."

I nearly lost it too as gunfire rattled the gusts of ash. "You have got to be kidding me ..."

Blue Ops troops. With some serious guns. They burst from the smoke like shadows, like –

Like something out of a video game.

Next thing, the smoky plaza was jumping with bullets flying off the marble.

"Drive!" I yelled, terrified, as I hid in the footwell of the passenger side.

Blink stepped on the gas. The engine roared but we didn't move.

The Blue Ops soldiers drew closer.

"We're still inside the game."

Vik said that.

I remember.

*"The UltraState's so hi-tech,
you can't tell what's real."*

Vik said that.

*Inside the UltraState
Inside the UltraState
Inside the UltraState*

Jeez, Vik.

*You were wrong ... but in a way,
you were right.*

CHAPTER 11

See No Evil, Hear No Evil

"It's not in gear!" I shouted at Blink. "Get your foot down on the clutch."

I jammed the jeep into first gear. The soldiers were almost on us, but then the jeep's wheels spun and at last we screeched away. Soldiers jumped aside as we stormed past them. Bullets fired again and again until Blink turned the wheel hard to fling us around the corner of a pyramid. I felt something hit my neck and fall to the floor. It must've bounced off my seat. I scooped it up.

"Rubber bullet," I shouted. "They're not trying to really kill us."

"Want me to stop so you can give it back to them?" Blink asked.

I shook my head. As I did, my ears crackled.

Oh, no ...

"We're still in the UltraState!" Vik shouted behind me.

Then my hearing died into thick silence. My ears even stopped ringing. The street bumped and jolted as Blink swung the jeep left. She shouted something but I couldn't understand. I pointed to my ears. Blink's eyes were full of terror. The jeep swerved at a wall.

Then Blink pointed to her eyes.

Oh my god, she's gone blind.

"Slow down! Left! Hard left!" I shouted, praying that I was saying the right words, praying she could hear me. She jerked too hard on the wheel. We smashed into a post box, knocked it over. I felt the jolt of the impact but heard nothing. "Steer right! Not so hard. More to the left – no! Right again!"

Blink gripped the wheel so tight the bones of her hands glowed.

I looked behind. Soldiers, still running. Still firing.

"Go faster!" I shouted – at least, I hoped so. "If the wheel's at twelve o'clock, now – then turn it to nine o'clock."

We lurched, she fumbled the gears, the jeep swerved at a wall.

"Whoa! Back to one o'clock! Slow down. Ten o'clock round this bend and swing back to twelve ... no, I said – twelve! Faster. Press harder on the gas."

It was a total nightmare. I couldn't hear, Blink couldn't see. I was shouting myself hoarse – but couldn't hear a word. I couldn't hear the jeep or anything around us. Blink was driving but she couldn't see where she was going. She was driving blind. Tears poured down her burned, sticky cheeks as she stared blankly out the broken windscreen. My nerves were in tatters.

"All right," I shouted. "The airfield is dead ahead. Go a bit faster, Blue Ops are still after us ..."

I had no idea if Blink was talking back, or if she could even hear me.

My sight sparked and flickered, like there was static in my eyes.

"No!" I shouted. "Come on! Faster, Blink ... We've got to reach that airfield!"

The streets zoomed past. I could see the planes on the runway, gleaming under the grey sky, but the image was cracking up. My eyes watered, stung. Bits of sound barked in my ears. It was a real effort to keep calm, stay in control.

With a spit of static, a truck – black with that blue star – roared out and swung into our path.

"Brake!" I could hear the terror in my shout now, as I braced for impact. "Hard right!"

Too late. There was a kind of sick grace to the crash as we hit the truck side on. I smashed my head. Blackness swooped in again.

When I opened my eyes I saw the planes 300 metres away. Blink couldn't see them – her broken face was jammed into the steering wheel.

Soldier Girl loomed over me. She was cool and calm, but her nose was still swollen from when Blink had hit her. She leaned over me, needle in hand. I kept my eyes on the planes ahead.

I felt the needle vampire into my vein.

Game over.

CHAPTER 12

All Senses Down

They say, don't they, that when you're near to death, it's like you're in a tunnel drifting towards a light at the end.

I could see the light. Only, it was coming towards me. It was burning into my brain.

A light held by Soldier Girl, as she looked into my eyes.

I turned away, blinking hard. *Blink.*

And Blink was there too. She was next to me, strapped to a hospital trolley. She had bandages

on the cuts and burns on her face, and she wore
a white cotton gown. The sort you wear when
you're about to have an operation.

I called to her, but no sound came. I realised
I was deaf still. I was in a white gown, like Blink.
The room was bright, the walls clear plastic with
darkness beyond. I could only imagine the smell
of antiseptic. A bank of computer servers and
monitors was all along the walls. Some of the
screens showed charts and numbers like in a
hospital, some showed grim landscapes I didn't
recognise. Rubble. Ruins.

Then my sight flickered. I looked up at
Soldier Girl. She gazed down at me, like a vet at
a sick animal.

She must have realised my sight was
going. I felt a scratch on my arm. I felt like I
was floating – as if I wasn't real at all. I was
becoming nothing, trapped in a dark and silent
world.

Then I opened my eyes and I was in a night-world full of rubble. I could smell smoke, and a cold, stiff breeze gave me goose bumps. I could hear the crackle of flames, and the howl of distant wolves. My mouth tasted stale like I'd just woken up.

Blink stood beside me.

We were in the apocalypse world from that UltraState game. *Pokko.* The one we'd played in the trials.

I looked at Blink. Her burns were healed and she looked good in her combat gear. The zombie-killing gun I held looked even better. I was armed. I was ready to fight.

"What are we doing here?" Blink said.

A zombie stepped out from the darkness. Its pale, rotten head lolled to one side.

"We're fighting," I snapped, aiming my gun at the zombie. "That's what we're doing here."

The zombie held up a hand as if for silence. "Fighting for your lives, yes. But not in the way you think."

The zombie sounded just like Soldier Girl.

"I'm speaking to you from the world of *Pokko*," she went on, "because your real-world senses are so damaged, you can no longer be reached in reality. You are in this world now."

I stared at her. There were so many things I wanted to say, but none of them would come out.

Blink got there first. "The UltraState did this to us?" she asked.

"Yes," said Soldier Girl. "We didn't know, of course, not straight away. UltraState causes total wipe-out of your senses." She paused. "If it's not treated, the wipe-out is terminal."

"We're dying?" Blink asked. "Everyone who took part in the trials?"

"Seventy people affected in total," the zombie Soldier Girl confirmed.

"And if we *are* treated?" I said. "That drink you gave us at the start, was it –?"

"The drink was made to ramp up the attack on your senses ... We hoped this would kick-start the body's own defences."

"And didn't *that* turn out well," Blink muttered. "*Not.*"

I remembered the man talking over the deaf and blind body of Next Door Girl in the hotel. "*It was always a risk, but the state needs pushing along ...*"

"If news of this ... problem got out, Sensia would be over. Huge pay-outs, no player confidence, court cases, fines ..."

"Better to murder us all then," Blink sneered. "Blow us to bits in the middle of our tournament – how did you plan to explain that away?"

"The city's power comes from a small nuclear power plant," Soldier Girl went on. Her zombie smile now looked more sad than evil. "Your friend Squirrel was a skilled hacker. We will say that she hacked into the nuclear power station and caused that blast ..."

I stared. "You'll blame it on her?"

"Maybe she made a mistake? Maybe she wanted to show off?" Soldier Girl went on. "Or maybe she couldn't bear to finish up at the bottom of the ladder yet again ..."

"Shut up!" I shouted, my throat as dry as dust. "You killed Squirrel, Vik ... Everyone!"

"The people whose senses were just too damaged were disposed of," Soldier Girl told us. "But in fact, Squirrel is alive – *just*. Something in Squirrel's body left her unaffected by UltraState. When we find out what that is, it will offer the best hope for a cure."

Blink snapped hard at her words: "You're gonna cure us?"

"If we can."

"But why?" Blink wanted to know.

"Think about it," I said. "Sensia's spent billions developing the UltraState. They need it to work after all the money they've invested."

"You will be treated here in secret," Soldier Girl went on. "In the meantime, your senses will be looked after in a new and improved UltraState world."

"Here?" I looked around with a chill of fear. "Do you mean we stay in a game? We fight to stay alive all the time?"

"No. We need to preserve the real you, not just a player in a game. And so we are perfecting a new simulation. You will stay in an UltraState version of Hotel Escape. If we can return you to your normal selves, you will leave here thinking you've had the greatest holiday of your life." Her jaw hung open in a nasty leer. "Because you are WINNERS."

And with that, Soldier Girl turned and walked away into the ruins. A cold wind howled. We were in our own apocalypse.

I turned to Blink. She stepped closer. We held each other, really, really tight.

I don't know how long we were there. It was game time, not real time.

My sight started to flicker.

"I don't think we have long now, Kenzie," Blink hissed. "Whatever happens, we have got to remember what they did to us. They can't get away with this. Remember Vik and Squirrel. Remember it all."

"We won't be able to." Tears burned the back of my throat. I gulped them away. "Sensia would never have told us if we stood a hope of remembering."

"Shut up! We *have* to remember." A white mist drew in. The sounds of this world stopped. It felt as if the ground was falling away. "K-Boy, if we get better, if they *do* let us go, we've got to bring down Sensia."

"Blink ..." I couldn't see her but I could feel her arms around me. "Theresa –?"

"We've got to tell the world, K-Boy!" Her voice broke. Broke up. "Remember! Promise me you're going to –"

Remember.
Remember, it's important.

Remember the UltraState
play-pod in the hotel lobby?

It was turned on.

And the cameras in the lobby
and the corridors.

Cameras filming from all angles.

Feeding the pictures into that
UltraState console.

Creating the world.
Creating our prison.

Realer than real.

*The good thing is, you'll be
seeing everyone again.*

Just as they were.

But you will remember.
Because Sensia can't get away with this.

Can't get away
Can't get awa
Can't get aw
Can't get a
Can't get
Can't ge
Can't g
Can't
Can'

CHAPTER 13

Sweet Smell of Success

I'd fallen asleep in the limo. What a waste! Tiredness had crept up on me. Back home it was midnight, but here it was only six p.m. 'So this is what jet lag feels like!' I thought, as I rubbed my eyes. I'd have to get used to long flights when I turned pro. Dreamhack in Sweden, QuakeCon in the US of A, Fragapalooza in Canada …

K-Boy would be mixing with the *big* boys.

The driver pulled my luggage from the boot like it weighed nothing and the hotel's glass doors slid open. I stepped inside.

What I saw refreshed me right away. Wow.

The massive lobby was cool in every way. It was made of nothing but metal and glass and you could have stood a rocket in there. Sparks of light – like fireworks frozen mid-blast, high above us – gave the space a soft glow while steel blinds turned the sun into thick bars of light. The floor was a grid of white marble and soft grey carpet. As I crossed it I felt like a counter in a board game. Ha, board games! Prehistoric next to what I could see bang centre in the lobby – a Sensia UltraState play-pod, the size of a sports car, pulsing green and good to go.

I stared at it. Something didn't feel right.

This girl was looking at it too. I couldn't help but clock the white patch from her cheek to her neck on her otherwise clear black skin. Shades on. Hair razored and quiffed. Mean lips. Cool.

"Do I know you?" I said. "Did I maybe see you someplace?"

"You wish!" she said, and then she turned and walked over to check in her bags.

I followed her, checking her out and smiling.

'K-Boy,' I thought, 'how'd you ever get luck like this?'

Something told me that the days ahead were going to be wild.

The sickest ever.

Our books are tested
for children and young people by
children and young people.

Thanks to everyone who consulted on
a manuscript for their time and effort in
helping us to make our books better
for our readers.